Pop-Pop Smells Funny

But We Love Him Anyway

Written by J.R. Buchta

Illustrated by Daniela Frongia

Pop-Pop Smells Funny; But We Love Him Anyway

Library of Congress Control Number: 2024904277

ISBN 979-8-9869895-4-9 (Paperback)
ISBN 979-8-9869895-5-6 (Hardcover)
ISBN 979-8-9869895-6-3 (Ebook)

JUVENILE FICTION / Family / Grandparents
JUVENILE FICTION / Humorous Stories

Illustrations and cover art by Daniela Frongia at caisarts.com
Interior and cover design by Michelle M. White at mmwbooks.com

Printed in Yardley, Pennsylvania, USA by Warbucks, Inc.

For more information, visit www.warbucksbooks.com

For permissions and bulk book orders, contact emily@thewonderfulonce.com

Yardley, Pennsylvania, USA

Dedicated to Grandfathers around the world

Everybody loves Pop-Pop!

Moms love Pop-Pop.

Dads love Pop-Pop.

Grandchildren love Pop-Pop.

Nothing will ever stop us from loving Pop-Pop.

Pop-Pop makes us smile and laugh...

even when he doesn't try!

That's because sometimes

Pop-Pop smells funny...

But we love him anyway!

Pee-Poo!

Pop-Pop changes a diaper.

Whoa!

Pop-Pop kicks off his shoes to relax.

LOOK OUT, Pop-Pop!

DON'T SIT THERE!

UH-OH!

Pop-Pop stepped in it.

Yuck!

Pop-Pop puts raw onions on his hot dog.

Whoops!

Pop-Pop forgot to brush his teeth today.

Heads up!

Pop-Pop takes a trip to the beach.

Yikes!

There's something fishy about Pop-Pop.

Ah-Choo!!

Pop-Pop wears too much aftershave.

RUN AWAY!

Pop-Pop used our potty.

Phew!

Pop-Pop goes for a jog.

What's *that* smell?

Pop-Pop pulled some weeds—and some muscles.

Oh boy!

Pop-Pop ate spicy meatballs for dinner.

Oh my!

Pop-Pop's favorite old sweater smells like mothballs.

EEK!

Pop-Pop meets a skunk!

Bon appetit!

Pop-Pop loves stinky cheese as a midnight snack.

WOOF!

Pop-Pop gives the dog a bath.

WHO TOOTED??

But we all know...

Pop-Pop smells best when he doesn't smell at all!

About the Illustrator

Daniela Frongia, also known as Caisarts, is a talented international children's book illustrator with over 14 years of professional experience. Born in Sardinia, Italy, in 1979, Daniela developed a passion for drawing at the age of 5, initially focusing on Disney characters before discovering the anime world.

After graduating from Art School and gaining various art-related experiences, Daniela made the decision to relocate to London, UK. It was in London that she held her first personal art exhibition, marking a significant milestone in her artistic journey. Embracing the digital realm, Daniela found greater flexibility in her work, allowing her to pursue her love of travel. With just her Wacom Cintiq, she can create art from virtually anywhere.

About the Author

J.R. Buchta, a.k.a. Pops to Mack, Coop, and Leo, was born and raised in Philadelphia PA. As a youngster, he expressed an interest in music and spent most of his early life in the performing arts as a singer-songwriter. After graduating from the University of Pennsylvania, he entered the business world and made a career in marketing for various entrepreneurial ventures. Today, he resides in Bucks County PA with his wife.

His interest in writing took a turn towards children's books when his grandchildren were born and he recognized the power of their imaginations and their enjoyment of reading. He is the author of the award-winning book *The Wonderful Once: A Christmas Story*.

54635517R00018

Printed at: Fri Jul 8 04:08:14 2016 on device lvoce05-52